Passing As "Straight"

Beautiful Women Whose True Sexuality
Went Undetected by a Judgmental Society

Compiled by

Celebrity Author Kinyatta E. Gray

Passing As "Straight": Beautiful Women Whose True Sexuality Went Undetected By A Judgmental Society
COMPILED BY: Celebrity Author Kinyatta E. Gray

© 2020

PUBLISHED BY: Pen Legacy® (penlegacy.com)
TYPESETTING & LAYOUT BY: Junnita Jackson (theliarscraft.com)
COVER DESIGN BY: Christian Cuan

DISCLAIMER

Author and Co-Author memories are not perfect, and information is being shared to the best of our knowledge. Identities have been changed to avoid legal pitfalls.

Library of Congress Cataloging – in- Publication Data has been applied for.

ISBN: 978-1-7333964-9-3

PRINTED IN THE UNITED STATES OF AMERICA.

Also by Kinyatta E. Gray

Books

30 Days: Surviving the Trauma and Unexpected Loss of a Single Parent as an Only Child

From Section 8 to C.E.O. (Available May 2020)

Table of Contents

Dedication

This book is dedicated to those who fully embrace themselves and who walk in their truth.
This book is also dedicated to those who fully embraced themselves, walked in their truth and have died.

People may hate you for being different and not living by society's standards, but deep down, they wish they had the courage to do the same.

~Unknown

Prologue

Sweat trickled down the side of her face, coupled with a sense of unease and absolute chaos. She could feel it within herself as it soared and roared with no opportunity to console the drowning feeling. Her palms became sweaty, her knees threatened to fail her, and her eyes hurt just by staring at the trio around the dining table as they ate happily.

They seemed happy, or at least, they understood the word in ways she dared not.

"Everything is going to hell if you do this", Jessica whispered to herself with clenched fists.

Gulping down hard, clamping her eyelids shut and taking shallow breaths, she approached the dining table with a raging heart and hurting ribcages. It was safe to say every single organ inside her felt her pain, and they wept with her soul as well.

"My baby is about to become a woman!" The woman Jessica held close to heart, her mentor and mother, extended her arm out to welcome her to the table.

Jessica managed a smile or something that felt like a smile as she placed herself into her designated seat, directly opposite the emblem of her torment over the past one-year.

She cringed just by looking at him, and suddenly felt overwhelmed by a disturbing sense of heat ravaging her insides.

Jessica cleared her throat, looked from her father to her ever-smiling mother, "Dad… mom… ehm… ".

Her lips wouldn't dare let off the words she intended to spill. It was the same way they failed her the night before when they all went out and she badly needed to confide in them. It was the same way they failed her when she pulled her mother to the side after vigil the night before, hoping to let her know or at least, set herself free from the mental and emotional torments that riddled her being.

Her father, the founder of one of the biggest churches in Houston, and a staunch believer in Christ grinned as he glared at Jessica. "Yes darling?"

The leering gaze riddled through Jessica and caused a troubling sensation to cradle down her spine. She gulped down saliva and several lumps of worries formed in her throat disturbingly. Her eyes blinked intermittently, and her feet began to tap on the floor underneath the table, as she grew anxious.

"You don't look so good, Jessica", her ever-sensitive mother asked with a raised brow.

Jessica cocked her head, tightened her fists on the table and looked at her mother with a reaching soul, wishing she would note the pain and anguish in her eyes and somehow just understand her plight.

"Come on baby, there is no harm in getting married", Arthur nudged his daughter playfully. "Your mother was in the same shoes as you when she wanted to get married to me".

Her father seemed so cheerful and happy, prompting Jessica to question what she was about to do. It was the impression of acceptance and gratitude which they showed her from the moment she brought James home about six months back that had kept her feeling "okay", even if she wasn't entirely happy.

Jessica looked at her husband-to-be and grinned. James smirked back and winked at her. Her heart felt sorry for him and for herself.

"Now I don't have to worry about watching other people's kids get married in the church while mine had never even brought home a man", Arthur giggled excitedly before reaching for his glass of wine and taking subtle sips from it.

"Come on Arthur", Jessica's mother nudged at her husband's arm, trying to warn him against embarrassing the Jessica in front of her man.

Arthur cleared his throat, looked to Jessica with so much pride and happiness glowing in his eyes. His wide smile was good enough to melt any worry and the way he gawked at Jessica made her desire this particular relationship she had with her father for as long as possible. Considering they couldn't breathe in the same air even if they were hundreds of feet from one another just a year ago, it felt marvelous and like a miracle to be dining on the same table with her father.

"We are so proud of you, honey", her mother rubbed her hand and smiled wildly before getting up to cut the honey roasted chicken specially made to commemorate her spending some days in their house with her husband-to-be, just weeks before their wedding.

Jessica sighed in tiredness, continued to clench her fists as she eyeballed her man who seemed ignorant of her plight. In that moment, thirty year old Jessica who was too worried about what her father, mother or everyone in the church community where she grew up would think about her and the true choice she needed to make at heart, sought the best way out from the mental turmoil she was battling with in that very moment.

"Oh, I cannot wait to see what cute babies you two are going to make", her mother chuckled.

Arthur raised his head, took a moment from his meal and said to his daughter, "Your kids had better have curly hair from my side of the family".

The trio burst out laughing, except Jessica who could feel her rage continues to soar and her tolerance level seriously threatened.

"Just imagine - those kids in school used to tease you about being gay", Arthur continued. "They have to wait some weeks more and we'll show them who is gay".

Jessica's face reddened, her resolve heightened and without notice, she rammed her fists into the table and fumed. "I am a lesbian!"

Silence engulfed the entire room and in specific, the dining table area. Chirping sounds from crickets could be heard clearly now and even the swashing sound of the wind as the tree branches danced melodiously to their tune.

"Now is not the time for motherfucking jokes dear", Arthur nervously chuckled as he broke through the silence and discarded his daughter's words.

Jessica's mother on the other hand continued to gawk at her daughter, saying nothing, but holding enough words in her head to make her skull explode.

"I am a lesbian", Jessica made it known once again, this time in lesser tone and with more conviction to get her message across.

Arthur stiffened his hand around his fork and slowly turned his head to pay attention to his daughter. The jovial, smiling and cheerful demeanor on this church-going man was no more.

"I am sorry, but I cannot continue with any of these charades", Jessica got up from her seat with reddened eyes. "I have waited for so long to let this out. I have wanted nothing but for you to see past everything and truly see who I am within and what I am".

Arthur remained silent, but his reddened eyes and tightened muscles did enough to air his feelings. Jessica's mother let go of the things in her hand, while James looked lost, whitened in the face and without an ounce of comprehension about what was going on.

Jessica turned to James with a heavy heart. "I am sorry I used you. I am sorry this is how I finally decided to come out".

James sniffed subtly, slid his seat backwards and shot up from it without a single word – while snatching the dozen roses he had given Jessica. The door slammed shut behind him as he disappeared into the night and out of sight for good.

Arthur was the next to stand to his feet. "You aren't my daughter. You were never my daughter and I always knew something wasn't right about you".

He slid his seat backwards, looked at his wife, Jessica's mother, and shook his head.

"You didn't give me a daughter… you gave me a disappointment and an abomination", the man said with the most distasteful tone he could muster.

Jessica stretched her hand towards her father and replied, "I'm a lesbian, not… ".

Arthur interjected in a deafening tone. "You aren't my daughter! You will never be my daughter! Get the hell out of my house!"

Jessica's heart slumped through her chest and sunk further into her stomach.

"I want you out of my house!" Arthur yelled.

The words pierced Jessica's chest, hard and precisely, severing every nerve within and causing her nothing but overwhelming emotions. It felt surreal that she had neglected her true self and desire to please the same man she referred to as her father, but who wouldn't accept her for who she was.

"I mean it!" Arthur whispered before disappearing from sight.

Warm tears flanked her cheeks and the bitter-salty taste they left on her lips prompted her forward. Each step forward came with immeasurable amount of pain. It had taken no less than thirteen long years for her to be true to herself, and it was all for nothing.

The endless pretense, endless lies and belittling deeds she took through two decades, in an effort to feel accepted, normal and never get tagged as an abomination ate at her dearly and haunted her soul with no reprieve in sight. Jessica hurried up the stairs and raced for her room. She had put everything in place, knowing full well her father was never going to accept her for whom and for what she was.

With the rope in place, a stool laid to rest just beneath the ceiling fan. Jessica took a step towards the only way she could attain freedom. By morning light, it would be over; the pretense, need to betray her true self and emotions, and the overwhelming need to please others so she could be accepted.

Glaring out the window with the rope wrapped around her neck, the three words she had tried to live by escaped her lips one last time. "Passing as straight".

It was all she wanted to do and it was exactly what she did for thirteen solid years. By morning, it was bound to be over for heartbroken and rejected Jessica, whose ordeal is no different from hundreds of thousands like her in the United States, as well as the millions around the world.

This is to everyone, who feels robbed of his or her true nature, in an effort to *"Pass As Straight"*.

Kinyatta E. Gray
Author, Celebrity Travel Influencer & CEO

Kinyatta E. Gray is a Best Selling Author, Celebrity Travel Influencer and CEO of FlightsInStilettos. Kinyatta wrote and published her first book in 2019, a memoir, called 30 Days: Surviving the Trauma and Unexpected Loss of a Single Parent as an Only Child.

Kinyatta's aspirations to become an author were as a result of a heart-gripping moment in her mom's final moments of life. She committed to honoring her mother's legacy by becoming a published author. Kinyatta's mother wanted to be a published author but passed away in 2018 before ever realizing her dream.

Kinyatta has acquired the support of the biggest talent in the entertainment industry to support her book. The celebrities who have conveyed support for "30 Days" the memoir are Yandy Smith CEO of EGL Magazine & TV personality, TV personality Antoine Von Boozier, CEO of New Jersey's largest radio station Time2 Grind, Madison Jaye, Celebrity Podcaster, Pilar Scratch, Celebrity Public Relations Expert, and Always Ask Asia, Radio One Personality, just to name a few.

Rising in success, Kinyatta's book has been featured on a variety of press outlets such as Urban Magazine, Medium, Mogul, IHeart radio and Pandora "The Madison Jaye Show" and Fashion Gxd Magazine.

Also, The Davi Magazine based in London has featured Kinyatta internationally.

Kinyatta's memoir was also a 2019 sponsor of "Christmas with Carol" hosted by Carol Maraj, mother of Hip-hop icon, Nikki Minaj.

Kinyatta will be releasing her 3rd book called From Section 8 to CEO in the summer of 2020.

Instagram: @kinyattagraytheauthor
Facebook: kinyattagraytheauthor
Website: kinyattagray.com

Facts of Femme Life

by Kinyatta E. Gray

Growing up, I was always praised for having both inward and outward beauty. When you're blessed with these natural qualities, people automatically become drawn to you.

My mom used to always ask me, "What is it like to be so pretty and have people looking at you with pleasure and always going out of their way to accommodate you? What does it feel like to have men tell you at every turn that you're beautiful? What does it feel like to be admired by women and looked up to by little girls?"

I never thought about it that much and I never considered that other women, who may have looked differently, experienced life differently – maybe even uncomfortably. I knew that most of my life, I had experienced a hint of preferential treatment in a variety of settings (like at work) because of my outward appearance – magnified by my sweet disposition and friendly personality. My friendliness was often mistaken for some form of flirtation – especially with certain men who weren't accustomed to women in my position being very nice and personable with them. I smile a lot and I make eye contact a lot – I could see how someone could innocently think that my energy was giving off a bit more.

It never was, though. Funny story, I met Hillary Rodham Clinton (yes the Presidential candidate and former Secretary of State) years prior and if you ever have a chance to meet her or her husband, Bill Clinton, they are known for their mesmerizing 3-second handshakes while looking at you directly in the eye. It makes you feel like you're the only person in the room if only for that moment. I learned that from Hillary Clinton and adopted that practice as my own.

In addition to the mesmerizing handshakes, I am a fiercely feminine woman. I'm the type of woman that loves all things pink, purple and aqua. I need all things to bling, sparkle and shimmer, and I wear stilettos –not just any stilettos – but Christian Louboutin. I carry the best designer handbags, wear high-end makeup like Nars and MAC, flaunt mink eyelashes and wear the best hair extensions that money can buy. To top it off, I am a lover of skirts, not just any skirt – form-fitting, curve-hugging pencil skirts.

This is how I showed up every day at work and in life in general. For these reasons, it was hard for anyone to think that I was anything but a beautiful, straight single woman waiting for the right man to put a ring on it.

My life was secretive because I showed up every day with a glow and smile and no one could ever figure out why I was so happy or who was making me happy.

The most confident of men would shoot their shot and I would always be polite and kindly decline their advances – leaving their pride intact. The chase was mystifying to them – they never quite understood why I would never give in to their bold and numerous advances or accept their offers for lunch and gifts.

I had a few girlfriends. The closest ones knew who the love of my life was, and the rest of them didn't and never bothered to ask about my love life. They were too busy telling me about theirs. All of my girlfriends were "straight", so this made it even more extraordinarily easy for me to conceal parts of my identity to the general public. I blended in nicely.

Oddly enough, on at least two occasions, two of my "straight" girlfriends actually tried to come on to me. One time specifically, one of my friends spent the night at my house. Normal right? She also slept in my bed with me. There was nothing wrong with this because there was nowhere else for her to sleep and I knew that I had no ill intentions. She was my friend -- I thought nothing of it.

In the middle of the night, I felt hands rubbing the small of my back. I lay there paralyzed – thinking I know this isn't what I think it is. So, then her hands started to inch closer to my inner thighs. I immediately sat up. I didn't want to make her feel bad, so I was like, I don't fool around with my friends AT ALL. She became very upset that I didn't accept her advances and the rest of the night was very awkward. I didn't sleep at all. When morning came, she left, and I didn't speak to her for several years. This saddened me but it also opened my eyes up to the fact that perhaps she interpreted the invitation to sleep over to be more than what it really was. So, from that point forward I became mindful of my actions and requests with female friends.

Nevertheless, I found her behavior and that of others to be way out of line, because the impression I received from their actions was that just because I am lesbian – I liked all women. That couldn't be farther from the truth. I have a "type" and more importantly, I have standards and boundaries. This is, but yet, another reason I preferred not to reveal my sexual orientation.

I didn't need or want female friends trying to explore their sexuality with me or objectifying me.

When it came to trying to conceal my sexual orientation from co-workers, most of the time, I made it a point to avoid hanging out and dining in areas that I knew my co-workers heavily frequented when going on dates with my love. I'm not talking about a few restaurants and local bars; I'm talking about an entire county in the state of Maryland. I did everything in my power to conceal a very major part of my life so that I could continue to be treated in a manner I had become accustomed to most of my adult life while at work.

This was my life for many years – through several secret same-sex relationships.

I was hiding this huge secret – primarily at work.

Over time, I began to hate hiding parts of my identity. I always declined social activities hosted by my office and colleagues because I didn't want my secret to be revealed. I grew tired of having to be careful and mindful of who might see my love and me and how they might treat me thereafter. I also hated that some "mystery man" (conjured up in other people's minds) was getting the credit for my happiness and well-kept appearance and lifestyle.

'Why didn't I just set the record straight' you may ask?

Well, there are several reasons such as:

- Fear
- Not wanting to make my parents feel uncomfortable

- ➢ Not wanting to be discriminated against
- ➢ Not wanting to be called terrible names like "dyke"
- ➢ Not wanting to lose my status/favor with my co-workers/supervisor
- ➢ Not wanting to be treated differently by people learning of that part of my identity
- ➢ Not wanting to be the butt of jokes
- ➢ Not wanting to be ostracized
- ➢ Not wanting to be chastised, and
- ➢ Not wanting others forcing their religious beliefs on me.

***

However, in 2017, this would all change. Years prior, I began dating the person who would become the love of my life. I was dating someone that saw themselves building a future with me and settling down as a family. I had found someone that wanted nothing more than to support me as I raised my two children.

Finally, someone wanted to put a ring on it – her.

Now that I had finally found true love, I had to make some very real decisions on how I would live the rest of my adult life with her as a married woman. Surely as a married woman, I couldn't continue hiding and avoiding -- just to keep from being exposed for whom I really am. After all, I loved her – and she certainly didn't hide me.

Those that I feared would not accept me -- had no real influence over my life anyway. In the grand scheme of things – they were dispensable, but why would I have to get rid of them just to be myself?

I also believed wholeheartedly that I had the right to live my life according to my convictions.

My mother (even with her deeply indoctrinated western Christian values) grew to love the only person that I deemed the love of my life. Her acceptance made my feelings of not being accepted by others, more tolerable. God – no matter your age, there's a small part of us that will always yearn for our parents' approval. I had at least that. Even my absent biological father accepted my love (after a bout of fake outrage), as well as a host of family members on my paternal side.

Their acceptance meant the world to me. I breathed just a little…

Their acceptance also made saying "yes" a lot easier.

On one lovely spring evening over my favorite dessert in my favorite restaurant, I said, "yes" to the love of my life. I would indeed be her wife. I knew that my heart would never ache, that my nights would never be lonely and that I would experience love and loyalty that you only read about in cheesy romance novels – but in my world, this shit was happening. I had found my forever and ever. I truly had nothing else to worry about. Plus, she was tall (WNBA physique to be exact), fine (Latino & Black) a little bit hood and a lot stable – I didn't even have to secretly lust for anyone else – every single need and desire was met by her.

As time went on and in a strange twist of irony, around the season that I was to be married, I was scheduled to start a new job weeks later.

This was exactly the fresh start that I needed. I no longer had to worry about returning to my job, being accosted for wedding pictures and wedding details about my new "husband". I didn't have to worry about how people would look at me if I did show them my wedding pictures and they saw I married a 'she' and not a 'he'.

(A well-meaning employee repeatedly sent me e-mails asking to see my wedding pictures because she knew I had been planning a dream wedding. After much thought, and realizing I'd never have to work in the office with her again, I said, "fuck it" and sent her my favorite wedding photo of my love and I. After she received that wedding picture showing that my 'husband" was actually my wife, I never ever heard from her again. I knew that she wouldn't have accepted my life – that's why for many years I concealed it from her. Nevertheless, I was glad I didn't have to return to that office again.)

I didn't have to worry about reporting any changes to Human Resources that would reveal the secret I was hiding. I was vastly popular and liked in my office so any hint of the secret I was hiding would have been essentially front-page news.

I could transition quickly, quietly and reappear as a gay married woman on my new job. Who was going to question me? There are laws to protect this shit now. I was safe. I could quit the straight girl act and be my authentic self on my new job.

I made the decision that I would start my new job and walk in my truth and no one would ever have to wonder or assume anything about me, because I decided to settle that shit upfront once and for all. My spouse meant that much to me and she was worth it. I remember the sense of pride I had completing the benefits paperwork and submitting my new marriage certificate. Who was going to say something to me? No one knew me to be anything other than what they saw on my marriage certificate and how I presented myself on my first day of work.

I completed my new employment paperwork with my proper title "Mrs." and in the line for the spouse, I included her name.

A weight had been lifted, or at least so I thought.

As immediately as I decided to walk in my truth, I experienced the backlash I so desperately tried to avoid. I did not only experience this backlash, but my mother who was a prominent member of her church (Praise and Worship Leader & Church Administrator) also experienced it. At the time, my mother felt a need to disclose my upcoming marriage to her church leaders. When this happened, she spoke of being in settings when other church members would make rude comments such as: "ain't no child of mine coming home gay" and "I wish my child would bring another man home" (knowing that her only child was in a same-sex relationship). Oh, and she told me exactly who made these comments and who shook their heads in agreement with the insensitive comments.

Others outwardly expected her to disown me and to not participate or attend my wedding.

She experienced a tremendous amount of hurt as a result of this backlash. She eventually stopped going to the church altogether – in an act of defiance in order to stand with me. She left the choir and stopped socializing with her church friends for an extended period of time. I was glad she stopped attending that church and resentful of how she was treated.

Sadly, however, she was so badly ostracized that she felt uncomfortable posting pictures of my wedding on her social media pages. Think about it -- her only child got married – and she felt that it was best to minimize that day – because of what her church felt about it.

I remember one day noticing this very real fact. I asked her about it and she avoided the question. Months earlier she'd given me her Facebook password and I thought long and hard about accessing her account and posting pictures of my wedding as if I was her with the most outlandish and supportive comments. LOL

I decided not to because I didn't want to disrespect my mom or cause her any more injury. I don't know what the true impact would have been – so I spared her of what may have been the equivalent of public humiliation.

I remember her sadness and how torn she was. It broke my heart that my mother had to experience this kind of treatment by her so-called "friends". Her entire life revolved around this particular church – the members were like "family" to her, yet they treated her like trash over my life's decision and her support of me. I vowed never to go to that church or any church like it.

Dear Church: Keep that same energy for other perceived "sins".

Note: Not all "Christians" act like that. I actually worked with a woman (on my new job) who was a Pastor's wife, and I felt myself wanting to hold back my truth when talking about family. I decided that I would talk about my wife as casually as she was telling me about her husband. She didn't flinch. She didn't cut the conversation off. She didn't shove her views down my throat. She showed me love, respect and admiration. From that moment forward we embarked on a solid friendship based on honesty and free of hypocritical judgment. She would occasionally give me a hug, which I always felt was her way to affirm that she was a safe person.

***

That wasn't all I experienced when I revealed I was getting married to my longtime companion.

An old friend who had witnessed my struggles in abusive and toxic relationships informed me (upon receiving my wedding invitation) that she "didn't support same-sex marriage" and for that reason, she declined an invitation to my wedding. I could hear the self-righteousness in her voice.

My heart was shattered. Not only did I want her to attend the wedding, but I also wanted her **to be a part of it** – a bridesmaid to be exact. How the fuck did I not see this coming? When did she start to feel like this? Was it after the first time she met my love, the 2nd, 3rd, 4th or 5th? Never in a million years did I expect that friend in particular to react to me in that manner. We shared some of the best laughs and some of the deepest darkest secrets. I was utterly confused because she was one of the friends in the inner circle who knew of my love. In that moment, I realized she merely tolerated us. Maybe she was even praying against us. Her heart changed towards me long before the day she had received my wedding invitation. It was probably more acceptable to her that I got my ass beat by an unfaithful man, then to be in a healthy loving relationship with an honest woman.

We stopped speaking, permanently, after almost 20 years of friendship. I immediately started to wonder, who the fuck else has something they needed to tell me?

I never expected anyone to change their beliefs, but I did wish that in that one moment in my life, I could have been surrounded by people who understood that the hole stomped through my heart during the many years I suffered, was now fully repaired and that my heart was beating again.

For these reasons I personally experienced and for many more, some women choose to conceal their true sexual orientation and pass as straight.

In the summer of 2017, my dream wedding went on as planned and those that loved and supported our right to happiness were present – including my beautiful mother and my father. Others who were invited (in their absence) had revealed to me how they really felt about us by being "no-shows". That hurt deeply as well because believe me, a bride knows who she invited to her wedding and she expects to see every face there. Their names were on the seating chart, their seats reserved – yet their chairs remained empty.

***

A year later, my mother tragically and unexpectedly passed away in 2018. She transitioned knowing that I (her only child, her only blood relative) would never experience the kind of relationship trauma I had experienced years prior. She left this world assured that she left me in good protective hands. I was glad that just a year before, she not only attended my wedding, but also was a major part of it; she saw me happy instead of hurting, and full of life instead of having it snuffed away and beaten out of me.

Moreover, the friend that I spoke of who declined my wedding invitation, attended my mother's funeral. I had not seen or spoken to her since the day she declined my wedding invitation. Through tears, she apologized for hurting me and for the hurt I was experiencing that day at my mother's funeral. I made the choice to forgive her, not for her, but for me. However, I will never forget.

Walking in your truth is hard, but once you decide to -- it is very liberating for most people. Those that are concerned about your happiness and your emotional well-being will stand with you. Period.

Love who loves you. Love who supports you. Love who stands up for you.

Sarina Mack,
Co-Author

Growing up in East New York, Brooklyn the only child of a strict Correctional Officer for a mother. Sarina Mack, M.Ed., LMSW is a Mental Health Clinician who has spent her life helping people grow, learn, and figure out their worth but she could not figure out her own. No longer in the grips of fear; she escaped despair, insurmountable obstacles, and circumstances that altered her mental and physical health. All of which was triggered by the stress of hiding her true self. She has traveled through many personal transformations to present a story of truth, transparency, personal growth, and self-discovery.

Sarina is the mother of three Kings, and she takes pride in raising them to be productive men. She enjoys helping other children reach their full potential as well. Although her calling from God is to help others; inside she was being stifled. While helping others find their truth, she was not living hers.

Sarina's journey to her truth took her through many trials and tribulations. Separating from her now ex-husband Sarina left Brooklyn, NY and relocated to Newark, DE., where she currently resides. Sarina only took trash bags full of clothes and her youngest son's crib. She had to sell some of her material objects in order to provide for her three sons. This is when Sarina began to realize how materialistic and shallow, she had become. Sarina was able to secure housing but was not always able to maintain it. During that decade one of her hardships caused her to be evicted and her sista-friend had to pay for her hotel stay. After funds ran out for the hotel Sarina and her three sons moved in with her mother in a two-bedroom apartment. This was a very challenging time in Sarina's life. Sarina having to move back in with her mother caused her to slowly die inside. Sarina needed to be resurrected. The will to provide a stable life for her three sons helped her see the light.

The road that Sarina traveled opened her eyes and she became more humbled and grateful than she could ever imagine. Sarina was eventually able to secure and maintain housing. She became employed at a very lucrative job. Things were starting to look up for Sarina. Now was the time for her to emerge!

Instagram: @thebutterflyemerges
Website: www.sarinamack.com

The Cocoon

by Sarina Mack

There is nothing on the exterior of a caterpillar that hints at the beauty it will become.

There is nothing about the beauty of the butterfly that hints at its hardening and the period of darkness and isolation it must endure for its wings to manifest, but oh, when they manifest.

At the age of 40, I discovered my wings....and I haven't stopped flying since.

It was Thursday, the 14th of September, the day that I walked into my new job; high-waist, wide legged slacks, five-inch pumps and cat-eye frames. I, Sarina was Ruby Woo fine. Mentally, I had prepared myself for this new beginning, the first day of a fresh start to rebuilding. Unbeknownst to me, by the end of that day, I would lay eyes on my future. I sat at my desk, setting up my new home away from home, when a voice, soon turning into the most infectious laughter, stopped me dead in my tracks. Being nosey, I peeked around the corner, catching sight of a smile that could light up any dark room. Like a moth to a flame, I was immediately drawn in. *Who was this individual? Did they work in my department? Should I introduce myself or was it too soon? Would I appear desperate, too obvious that they had my attention?* Dayummm, what was a girl to do? Mind racing, heart pounding, there was no way I could just lay low.

A simple "Hello" was all I was able to muster up on that day, but I wasn't going to let another day pass without making my move. Although we did not work in the same department, I was able to lay eyes on them the next day. On that day I came up with some reason to give them my number. I was so close to HER that I could smell the scent of HER perfume, which enhanced my desire to go the full distance to pursue this woman. It was probably one of the weakest come on lines that one could say, but HEY, it worked for me. Two years later, guess who is still by my side and hasn't let go of my hand since that day? It took us about two weeks to connect after I slid my number and shot my shit. Eager and excited to learn more about one another, our phone conversations lingered into the wee hours of the morning like two teenagers, knowing that we would eventually see each other at the office in just a few hours. After about two weeks, we finally decided to hang out. One thing you should know about me, is that I portray boldness like no other, fearing next to nothing. Just below the surface, I'm an introvert at heart; but according to societal demands to put a title on you. I am considered an ambivert. My eccentric style gives the perceptions that I'm extremely outgoing, love to party and be all up in the mix. In all actuality, I prefer to stay at home, in my bed with the remote in hand. During this initial stage of courting, I'm learning that while my person and I have so much in common, there are more aspects that assure me that I'm the Yin to their Yang.

Born and raised in a Philadelphia housing project, my person is one of three siblings, one living and the other, watching and protecting from above. A natural basketball star, her skills afforded her basketball scholarship to college, after which, she went on to serve in the U.S. Army for 19 years and counting. By the age of 17, she had already found comfort in living in her truth and knew exactly whom she wanted to love. I, on the other hand, grew up as an only child in Brooklyn, New York. I lived in a gated condo community and attended Catholic school my entire life. The most active thing I've ever done was cheerleading during high school. The most distinct difference is that I am a mother of three sons (ages 19, 13 and 9 at that time) and she has none. "How would this work?" I've asked myself several times.

Despite the fear of having to tell my sons that their mother had fallen in love with a woman, I continued to actively pursue Shamina. Shamina and I shared our very first kiss about three weeks after we started talking and the chill that went through my body was one that I would never forget. I remember saying, "Dayummmmm and she can KISS!" We both laughed, me more out of mere embarrassment than anything and her out of pure shock that I said that aloud. The more time I spent with Shamina, the more I knew that this was what I wanted and where I wanted to be.

I remember one day; Shamina and I were talking, and I said to her, "Once I give you some, you are my girl!" Shamina didn't believe that. Because I'd only dated men before her, she was positive this would just be a fling for me. Now, look at us talking about marriage and blending households. I guess I fooled her!

Who was I really fooling though? I thought by not allowing Shamina in the house, confining our talks to the safety of only the car or her home, that my sons were totally oblivious to our relationship. Little did I know, my three sons had already spoken amongst themselves about our "secret" relationship.

I remember the day like it was yesterday.

"I need you to be honest with me," my oldest son said to me.

"I am always honest," I replied.

Bluntly, D'Ondre asked, "Who is this DIKE chic you've been hanging out with?"

"Dre, dike is derogatory, and a very offensive word, so please refrain from using such language when you are talking to me. She has a name and her name is Shamina and she's my coworker."

Disbelievingly, Dre asked, "So, she's not your girlfriend or anything Ma?"

I was adamant. "NO! She's just my coworker."

Dre was not convinced. "She doesn't look like the 'type' of co-worker you would hang out with." Seeing right through me, Dre continued. "My brothers (Donovan and Dylan) and I had a talk and we are all convinced that she is your girlfriend. This is the happiest we've seen you in the last 10 years. Ma, if she is your girlfriend, it's okay!"

Like the punk I am, I started crying. Seizing the opportunity to free myself and be honest with my sons, I finally said, "Dre you are right; she is my girlfriend!" My sons had given me permission to LOVE... freely and unapologetically!

Now, I only had to tell my favorite girl, my first best friend, MY MOMMY! My mom is one of the coolest, most down to earth women/moms you could ever lay your eyes on. Telling my mom that I was dating a woman was easy breezy. My mother's response was simply, "Be careful; them bitches are crazy Nena!" That was all she had to say. She accepted me, Sarina, her only daughter. They say a mother knows her child and she knew me like no like other. With that said, it was that much easier for me to fall in love with Shamina, to finally tap into feelings I had tucked away so long ago.

Years prior, as a 20-year-old college student, I met a woman 11 years my senior, named LP who I knew was "in the life". I started having feelings that I had never felt for a woman before. I wanted to try, but I was hesitant. LP was everything I needed and wanted in that season; she was everything I was not. Just like Shamina, she was the total opposite of everything I was and stood for. It WORKED in my heart, but my heart was overthrown. I was BOLD enough to come on to her, but wasn't BOLD enough to stay. I gave in. I discarded the feelings I felt for this woman and allowed society to dictate what I had to do.

Longing for the whole perception of what was deemed the "picture-perfect household," you know: the husband, the kids, the dog and the "white picket fence," my desire to live society's dream brewed in my spirit. At 21, I met my now ex-husband. It was love at first sight! Sweeping me off my feet, we were married and by the age of 26, I had checked off society's "To-Do" list; I was married, had two kids, a home and a dog. He was everything I needed (well that I thought I needed) and then some. My ex-husband and I were legally married for 14 years, but separated for 10 of those years. My marriage lasted as long as we could make it last. I believe we just outgrew each other and wanted different things by that point in our lives, so we went our separate ways, but managed to co-parent healthily and communicate greatly.

After leaving my husband, I took a two-year break from dating to heal and reacquaint myself with Sarina. I was in school fulltime and working fulltime. Eventually, I met another gentleman and ultimately, we were in a relationship for six years. I loved him, but was never in love with him. This was a relationship of convenience. Between my ex-husband and my six-year relationship, I experienced everything a woman could desire in a man. However, there was something still missing. Wouldn't you think that after 20 years collectively of having all of this, that I would have been satisfied? But no, not me, I was not satisfied! I knew that something was missing. I eventually started fantasizing more about being with women. I yearned for the touch of a woman.   My urges for women intensified, but I still battled with myself on whether I would act on them. At the time, I would have never let anyone in my life know about these urges. The fear was so deep that I could not tell my besties, Murray's (since 1st grade), Shameka (since 3rd grade) and Gail (since high school) out of fear of losing the friendships; of them thinking that I was attracted to them, which I never was. I was unhappy with myself, with him, with everything that was in my space. I felt evil, mean and simply put, broken. I was still not being true to myself and, as a result, the relationship became stressful...so I left.

Still living a lie, I met another gentleman. We loved each other, but love was not enough. We both came with baggage and the relationship became extremely toxic, lasting only for one year, because I left, yet again (as you see, I have a habit of leaving).

In July of 2017, I lost my favorite guy in the entire world to Alzheimer's, Mi Abuelo (my grandfather, Antonio Alvarez Sr.). During that time, I started going through a transition. I started releasing anything/anyone that was unhealthy in my life. For three months, I isolated myself from the world, working on who I wanted to be and shedding who I had pretended to be. I needed to be free of the cocoon I had been trapped in for the last 19 years. I prayed. I cried. I screamed. I cut and colored my hair. I changed how I dressed; I no longer wanted to look like every other woman from New York. I wore labels to satisfy a need, to satisfy my brokenness, to make me feel complete because I was lacking something else. I wanted to arrive, I wanted to be present, I wanted to be available; I wanted to give myself the chance to heal and feel. I wanted to be set FREE! The funny thing about going through this transition of setting yourself FREE is, everyone takes it personal and makes it about them, when it's solely for the individual that wants and needs to be free. It's not because of a man, well a woman in my case, why I decided to isolate myself; but rather because it's a journey I believe one must do alone.

I had the whole summer to myself to go through this transition, which would bring me to that wonderful Thursday morning on September 14th, the day I laid eyes on the love of my life. During this break from everyone, I knew that I was reborn.

I had suffered for 19 years and didn't want to suffer any more no matter whom I lost in the process; and man… did they fall the fuck off. Though we had maintained our friendship up until that point, my ex-husband did a complete 180 once he learned of my relationship with

Shamina. He filed for divorce, became disrespectful and a distant father. Soon after, I also lost my relationship with the man who had helped my mother raise me for 11 years, a Sunni Muslim who firmly believed homosexuality to be haram (forbidden). This man, whom I called Daddy, had three biological daughters (younger than me) and one biological son (two years older than me), and then there was me. Already struggling to find my place in his life because I was not his blood, I knew that if the little shit I had done throughout the years (like having my first son out of wedlock) was enough to strain our relationship, then my newfound love would surely be reason for him to completely disown me. Surprisingly, the three young women who once called me Big Sister, would not be here either, especially the daughter who was right under me, who I saw come out of her mother's womb. She was my first baby, the baby sister I never had! Sadly, all ties to the Abdur-Rahim's were severed. Funny thing is that I'm totally okay with losing all of these relationships in order to free myself and stay with the love of my life.

After all, there were still the two besties (the other bestie and I were going through our own personal transition at this time) and my one male cousin, House, who mattered to me. Just like my mom, telling the besties was painless. My sista-friends continued to love on me the same way they loved on me prior to me telling them; but of course, there are always some welcoming jokes; that only a bestie could make. Eventually, within the next two years, that bestie and I made our way back to one another and she too accepted Sarina for who she had become.

It was House who I struggled to reveal the newly embraced Sarina to. How would I tell him? I felt like I was about to tell my dad and was, pretty much, shitting my pants. By that point, I was about nine months in deep with Shamina, so, I cowardly told him over a video chatting app. He was like, "Wait, what did you say? How are you gonna casually say that?" He had questions; he didn't understand.

Sensing his disappointment, I expressed to him that he was the last one who mattered to me and that if he couldn't accept me choosing to LIVE vs EXIST anymore, then it showed the depths of our relationship. I knew deep down he was still struggling, but his LOVE for me wouldn't allow him not to fuck with me anymore. Despite losing the other relationships, I still came out a winner!

The length of time it takes for a butterfly to emerge from its cocoon is dependent upon the environment around it. I knew that my transformation was going to be great, because it was time. Life had prepared me for that fateful day, that day that SHE walked into my life, that day that I was bold enough to shed my 19-year-old encasing and love who I wanted to love.

I no longer cared about the matters of this judgmental world. I realized that I merely existed, and it was time for me to emerge, showing all of my proud colors, and fly...maybe even soar.

The butterfly is now present! My Mina, as I call her, helped me FLY. She allowed me to be me. She didn't try to make me someone I was not, or that I thought I was. She helped me find my authentic self. Mina... The love of my life... My soon to be wife... Not my first female kiss, but she will be my everlasting kiss... My forever crush... My best friend… has not only saved my life, but the lives of my sons. We are a family… the purest, most organic meaning of family… and not the conventional / traditional family that the world wants to see, but we are a family; one happy "Gay" family. I now understand who I am, always was and have become.

Amanda Ri'Chard,

Co-Author

Michigan native, Amanda Ri'Chard moved to Washington D.C in 2012 to begin her career in public health and emergency management. Her career has allowed her to educate communities about necessary health issues and afforded her many opportunities to work alongside dedicated health professionals across the country. One of her greatest aspirations is to write books focused on various public health topics for children and adults to better understand public health issues and crises. This opportunity to co-author has given Amanda the necessary resources and tools to begin moving toward her future book venture. Amanda is also a practicing Catholic who has battled with her sexuality and moral teachings of the church. She knows, regardless of whom she loves, God will always love her and choose her to follow him. She has raised her five-year-old son to follow Christ and to always accept and love others regardless of their ethnicity, religion, and whom they choose to love. Amanda is so excited about this opportunity to share her story with you.

She says. "Always remember, God created each and every one of us in His image. You are not a mistake. You are amazing and you are loved."

Instagram: @AmandaRRichard
Twitter: @AmandaRRiChard

Readjusting My Crown

by Amanda Ri'Chard

To this day, I still love the sweet wood-burning smell of frankincense and myrrh. The scent is very calming, relaxing and one that covers me in peace. The feeling is very similar to the Catholic Church services I attended every Sunday where I grew up in Michigan. An hour filled with unified traditional hymns, a very quiet service, no shouting and a lot of time for silent prayer. Growing up Catholic, I attended mass with my family every Sunday and since I also attended Catholic school, I attended mass once a month with my class and sometimes more often for religious observances and funerals. Two of my favorite parts of church were the smells of the incense and completing some of the seven sacraments throughout the years. Growing up, I would watch as the priest walk around and purify the congregation with the frankincense held in a thurible. During sacred services, the priest walks around the church to a beautifully sung hymn as we all do the sign of the cross and pray to Our Father in Heaven to forgive us for our sins.

As a studious catholic student, I studied all seven of the sacraments, which include baptism, first communion, reconciliation, confirmation, marriage, holy orders and the anointing of the sick. All of my classmates and I were baptized, but I was the only student who had not received my first communion; it was an exciting time for me. I remember getting a white dress that went to my calves, a white veil that dropped to the middle of my back and a new rosary my grandmother handed to me in a pearled pouched. I still have that rosary and pouch 20 years later. On the day of my first communion, I not only received for the first time, the blood and body of Jesus in the form of unleavened bread and wine, but I also received my third sacrament, the sacrament of reconciliation. This sacrament teaches us about asking God for forgiveness, no matter how big or small our sins are. In third grade, I did not think of any "real" sins to ask forgiveness for of God. Instead, my reconciliation was focused on being a better sister, doing better on my homework and waking up on time so I wouldn't be late for school. As I got older, requesting forgiveness from God became a battle within myself and much deeper than my third-grade angst.

In middle school, my friends and I would put pictures of our celebrity crushes in our lockers. We had members of N'Sync, lil Bow Wow and B2k cut up into hearts on both the inside and outside of our lockers. One day, I cut out a picture of the lead singer of the girl group, Cleopatra. I thought she was absolutely beautiful. I would sing her songs all day long and speak about how badly I wanted to meet her. My friend asked who I wanted to meet more, the girl from Cleopatra or a member of B2K. I said Cleopatra. Why?

The stares I received made me feel uncomfortable and questioned what I had just said. Is it wrong that I find her beautiful? I still had crushes on the boys, but is what I am feeling a crush on girls too? I began realizing I had crushes on multiple girls my age and I was scared to share it with anyone. Our next sacrament was coming up and I was unsure if I could receive it if I was possibly bisexual.

The sacrament of confirmation is when we make the decision to continue in the Catholic faith and say, "Yes, I choose this faith. Yes, I want this faith. Yes, I am committed to this faith and I am working to be more Christ-like every single day." My classmates and I each chose a saint to inspire us to be more Christ-like as we took on this journey. I selected Saint Teresa of Avila for many reasons; the main one being; she was ridiculed in her younger life and was judged and deemed herself a miserable sinner. She looked to God and became dedicated to a life of following Christ. I felt if I shared my feelings for women, I would be judged and maybe if I focused on God more, I may be forgiven for my sin. On the day of my confirmation, my sponsor placed her hand on my shoulder as the monsignor prayed to God, calling on St. Teresa of Avila to help me walk in my journey to serve the Lord. As he placed the ashes and oils on my forehead in a thumb print version of the sign of the cross, I felt a warmth come over my body. I felt that at that moment, God had forgiven me for my intimate thoughts about women. It was as if I had begun a new life where those thoughts would erase from my mind and I would be focused on, one day, achieving my fifth sacrament, marriage.

I graduated high school in June 2006 and enrolled in a small college not too far from home. I was so excited to move into a dorm and experience life as a college student. When I arrived on campus, I saw so many beautiful faces. The feelings and thoughts I had suppressed since eighth grade had resurfaced. I could no longer control my thoughts and my feelings and needed to figure out how to explore them. There was only one person I could confide in, my college boyfriend. He and I would often talk about whom on campus we had crushes on and would possibly engage in a threesome with. The more we would talk, the more he heard my excitement and thrill to finally touch a woman. However, figuring out who and how, was the obstacle. Randomly, one night, while my boyfriend and I were drinking wine coolers, I received a text from one of my female friends. Her text read, "You can say no if you want, but I have the biggest crush on you and your boyfriend. If you two want to come over and have a threesome, please come." I dropped my phone in disbelief. She was a friend, a very beautiful, fun friend who I would have loved to explore my desires with. My boyfriend told me it was entirely up to me; and I said, "Let's go."

As we traveled to her home, my heart was pounding out of my chest. I was nervous as hell. All the years of waiting and wondering were finally here. *Would I enjoy it? What if I don't?* When we arrived to her front door, it was unlocked. I told him to go first, in case I changed my mind and wanted to bolt for the door, but I didn't change my mind. We entered her bedroom; she lay naked on top of her sheets, with her eyes staring directly at me. The comforter was on the edge of her bed; my boyfriend moved it to the floor. He looked at me and said, "Do I have your permission?" I said, "Go ahead," but I wasn't even looking at him. I stared at her as her beautiful body lay on the bed like a painting. She looked calm and I wanted nothing more than to kiss her full lips. So I did. The sex between us was amazing. Although I loved my boyfriend, the passion and sexual fulfillment she gave me exceeded any type of feeling I had received from men. After that experience, she and I began having sex regularly, just the two of us. We were still good friends, with a secret that nobody else knew. Nobody else could understand. When we would pass each other in the library, or at a party, we would wink at each other. If we ran into each other in the bathroom, we would give each other compliments. It felt good, but we both knew we couldn't tell anyone. We both had boyfriends and needed to keep this relationship we created private, until we had to let it go when she graduated. I continued fantasizing about the relationship and wished I could have a relationship that feels that good and not have to hide it. Then it hit me, I may be hiding it from my loved ones, but God sees and knows everything. I needed to go to confession.

A confessional is a small room in a church where the priest sits and waits for us to come and share our sins with him and ask for forgiveness from God. I walked into the confessional and knelt down behind the screen, so the priest could not see me, only hear my sins. I told him I had sinned and it had been however long since my last confession. He asked me what my sin was. I said "Father, I have had sex with a woman. And I enjoy her. I don't feel as if the feelings I have are wrong, but I have been taught that same sex relationships are immoral." The priest said, "The world is filled with many judgmental people, but Christ is not one. If we are working to be followers of Christ then we must do what Christ did. We walk in love with everyone regardless of whom they love or want to be with." The priest explained that no matter whom I end up with, God loves me and I am always welcomed in church, and that many people need to understand that. Because two people of the same sex cannot make a child, it is considered a sin. He said the sin I hear from you is engaging in premarital sex and that I needed to ask forgiveness for that and to remain pure until I marry. He added that God would judge us all on judgment day. After that, the conversation ended, I thanked the priest and went back toward the altar. I knelt down in a pew, did ten Hail Mary's and prayed in silence. I did not pray for God to deliver me from my sexuality, but instead for others to be more like the priest; to understand Jesus loved everyone, even if they were different than He was. As I knelt down, I looked up at a painting of Jesus on the cross. He looked beyond exhausted, sad and lifeless. Sweat and blood covered His body and a crown of thorns sat upon His head. This man who we all love was made a mockery of. I wanted to be more Christ-like and not let the fears of judgment overshadow who I am as a person. I stood up and readjusted my invisible crown and walked out of the church.

In May 2010, I graduated from undergrad and moved back home to begin grad school. Two years later, I graduated with my master's degree and decided it was time for me to spread my wings and move away. I was offered a job in Washington, D.C., a place I had never been, until it was time to move and begin this next chapter of my life. During my first year in D.C., I met people from all over the country and the world. It was a place that was filled with so much culture and individuality; I had never felt a sense of belonging until I moved there. I was able to date men and women openly and nobody seemed to care. I was still hiding it from all my friends and family back in the Midwest, until I met a very special woman that made me feel love in a way I hadn't before.

When we spoke on the phone, her voice made me happy. When we would go on dates, I would just stare at her, even if she weren't looking back. After months of dating, she told me she loved me. The kisses she gave me and the feeling of security were unmatched. When she asked me to be her girlfriend, I thought, *oh my goodness. It's happening. I have found the most amazing person and she's mine.* I, of course, told her yes, and we both smiled as we laid on the couch binge watching our favorite shows. It was casual, yet felt so perfect. My son even loved being around her; they began a special relationship of their own.

My son was three and a half years old during this time, which meant he had no filter and didn't know when to stop talking about mommy's personal business to everyone who would listen. I guess he assumed if it's happening in front of him, its fair game to share. Because of his extremely social and talkative nature, I knew it was time for me to come out before he outed me. So in true Amanda fashion, I sent a text. Yes, a text. I had previously sent a text to announce my pregnancy back in 2014 and thought; *hey it worked out fine; let me do it again.* This way, people can read it, process it and get back to me if they want to talk about it. A text for me is less awkward than sitting on the phone in silence. So I did it. I texted my loved ones and then turned the phone over as if I was shutting out the reactions. It was the most nervous I had ever felt. I wasn't ready for the disappointment and the beginning of the end of friendships, but that did not happen. I received texts of support and 'when can we meet her' texts. I received a few facetime calls with my best friends saying 'Are you serious? I can't believe you never told us!' The majority of the reactions were surprisingly positive. There were a few people who questioned my sexuality and how was I going to continue being Catholic, a mother and marry one day if I am with a woman. Some even assumed this was a phase due to bad break ups with men. My answer then is the same as it is now. "I am a Catholic, God-fearing mother. I know who I am and so does God. I try every single day to grow closer to God and cultivate a relationship with Him and my son. I have had many successes in life, and my sexuality does not take away from that." I once again readjusted my crown, picked myself up and continued to follow Him. I have raised my son to treat everyone with love and respect and I expect the same in return. We attend church, most Sundays, and will continue to grow towards God, regardless of who I choose to love. Some people may not understand, but God made me just like he made everyone else. I was once confused about my sexuality, but I am no longer hiding it. I am no longer confused. God knows my heart, my dedication and me to my faith. He pushes me to be a better person every single day, and to continue to focus on the most important aspects of my life. With God as my leader I know I will continue to succeed in life and wear my crown with dignity and strength. I also continue to follow in the footsteps of my confirmation saint. St. Teresa of Avila is a great writer of faith and prayer. She continues to inspire me, which is why I am able to write about my faith and share this part of my journey in this book with all of you.

"Bette Porter", Co-Author

Note: This co-author has chosen to remain anonymous. "Bette Porter" is her pen name.

"Bette Porter" is an educator, counselor, and life coach. As a high school student, "Bette" was heavily involved with her neighborhood elementary school and daycare where she spent her extra time as a volunteer. That's where her love for children sparked. Since then, her career and community involvements have all centered on the growth, development, and empowerment of young people. "Bette" is also an international traveler. She has traveled to over 20 countries and four continents. Although all of her travels are recreational, "Bette" makes every opportunity count through her philanthropic endeavors. Whether it's providing school supplies to kids in Ghana, teaching an English lesson in Zanzibar, or cleaning a devastated village in Bali, "Bette" always finds a way to give back to those in need. "Bette" is the founder of "Rhymes 'N Reason", a therapy program that uses music to heal. She is currently creating a 501C3 organization that will provide international travel opportunities to underprivileged youth in her community. Because of her community involvement and initiatives, "Bette" has recently been nominated as a "Top 40 Under 40". Her motto is "To the world you may be one person; but to one person you may be the world."

"Bette Porter" may be contacted via email at:
rhymesinreason@gmail.com

From the Closet to the Pulpit

by "Bette Porter"

I first knew that something was different about me when I was in the eighth grade. Unlike my friends, I never thought about boys. I didn't care who was fine, who dressed the best, or who liked me. To be honest, I wanted to be more like them. I wanted to dress how they dressed and act how they acted. There was always a boy trying to get with me, but I just wanted to play basketball with him. That's what I cared about: basketball and making my parents and grandparents happy.

So, in the ninth grade when my parents told me that I couldn't play basketball anymore, I was devastated. I was their "angel" child. I made good grades and didn't get into any trouble. So why was I being punished? They didn't take away the dance team or homecoming. Why basketball? According to my parents and grandparents, playing basketball in middle school was fine, but high school basketball was for "dykes" and "bull daggers"; not their "pretty little princess". So instead of speaking up for myself, I just surrendered to their vision for myself.

It wasn't until the 10th grade that it first happened. I was working at a local restaurant. I've always been a friendly person and although I've had several boyfriends, I was always more comfortable around my female friends than with boys. I was more relaxed, natural, and my true self. So on this particular day, there was nothing unusual about my female coworker and myself hanging out behind the kitchen when should've been on the floor. What was unusual was the feeling that encompassed me when she asked if I had ever kissed a girl. Why would she ask ME that? I didn't "look" gay. Did I do something to show my inner thoughts? The truthful answer was no. But what would happen if I told her the truth? Would she assume I wasn't interested and walk away? I was very interested, so should I say yes? Would that make her more comfortable to proceed? In that millisecond of time, many thoughts have crossed my mind but nothing came out of my mouth.

When her lips touched mine, I immediately felt guilty. Like I had done something wrong. I mean, that's what I had been taught. As the granddaughter of a prominent preacher, church was my life! I was there daily:

On Sundays we started with Sunday school. Then we would have regular church service followed by an afternoon or evening service in a neighboring city. On Mondays, I attended Missionary meetings with my grandmother. On Tuesdays, I was at youth choir rehearsal with my cousins or adult choir rehearsal with my parents. Wednesdays were for bible study. Thursdays was another choir rehearsal. "Friday Night Lights" were meant to keep us away from "the devil's world", and Saturdays were for whatever my grandfather came up with to get us there seven days straight. My life was at church!

There wasn't a day of the week I wasn't at the house of God! That's the main reason I wanted a job…I needed a break from church. Now, the church is my job! Go figure!

That first kiss behind the kitchen at my job ignited my attraction for women, but because of my religious upbringing, I hid my desires. My parents caught wind of it my senior year in high school. They felt like I was too close to one of my "friends". They accused her of being gay and restricted my interactions with her. There was no way their homecoming queen, prom queen; debutante daughter was going to be associated with "a girl like her". My parents became weary of every female relationship I had to the point where I could not have any female company or hang out with any female friends. However, they didn't have any problems with male interactions. Yes, I had boyfriends in high school, college, and even as an adult but none of it felt natural. It was all forced because "that's how it's supposed to be." Also, for my parents and grandparents sake.

Although I've never had girlfriends, there was always a girl behind the scenes. Truthfully told, I've been physical with more women than men. While in college, although I still lived with my parents, I became a little more rebellious. The way I dressed changed, I begin to argue with and defy my parents, and I was sneaking around with girls. Their biggest fear was the world finding out they had a gay daughter. So their concern remained in-home. They never spoke about their assumptions with my grandparents or any other family member. But they told the whole world about the boys I dated.

During my freshman year in college, I began to fall in love with an older mentor of mine. She had become my mentor when I was in the 8th grade. She was like my big sister and in some cases, a mom. Although I never said the words "I'm gay" to anyone. She was the first to know about my girl on girl interactions. She was my confidant and my best friend. Everything I looked for in a mother, she provided. With her, I could be my true self. I didn't feel judged or guilty about my feelings. I kept my actions secret from my closest friends but there was nothing about me she didn't know. In high school when my parents restricted me from being around girls outside of family and church, she was one of them. They didn't allow me to hang out with her anymore; however, we spoke on the phone daily. Although we had a close relationship and she knew everything there was to know about me, I knew very little about her. She did not disclose to me much about her personal life. So at the beginning of my second semester in college, I finally built up enough courage to tell her about the feelings I had begun to have towards her. I was overcome with emotions when she admitted to me that she was bisexual. Part of me was elated! It made sense to me why she was so comforting and understanding about what I was experiencing. Another part of me was mad as hell! Why wouldn't she tell me this before? Here I am thinking I'm the only one like me (feminine and gay) and here her gay ass is with her high heels and makeup and hair on point! In my mind, all gay women were masculine and something was wrong with me because I wasn't masculine…just a bit of tomboy though.

About a month after our revelations, she and I began a four-year relationship that was complete with every emotion known to man, primarily guilt. My guilt stemmed from my wholehearted belief that God was unhappy with me, and hers, from getting romantically involved with her mentee (I was 19; she was 27). Besides that, our relationship was amazing! It was our little secret. For similar reasons (church, jobs, family), neither of us were open about our sexuality nor our relationship. Everyone just thought we were just really close. We were passing as straight! Behind closed doors, we were heavily in love. Although we weren't each other's first, we both experienced a lot of firsts with each other. She was still like my big sister and she still filled in voids that I wish my mom would've. She was my lover and my friend. I was her Whitney Houston and she was my Robyn Crawford! With her, every need was fulfilled. During this time, she and I both continued having relationships with other people (men and women). I know that sounds crazy, but that was our relationship. There was no jealousy or relationship drama. I was a young, college student exploring my sexuality and she understood that. She was older and gave me everything I needed physically and emotionally. We were each other's "cake and eat it too".

Regardless of how hard I tried, I could not overcome the guilt that my religious beliefs had on me. My guilt was affecting me physically. Even my grandparents noticed. Of course, I couldn't tell them the truth. I just blamed everything on school and work. I finally decided to end all of my physical relationships, including the one with my mentor. She understood and we continued to have the close-knit relationship we had always had, minus the physical part. So from that point on, my focus was finishing school, work, and church.

Once I graduated high school, I stopped attending my grandfather's church as often as I had before. I started going to church with mentor and became heavily involved with them. That church made me feel more comfortable than the one I grew up in. This church taught me more about having a relationship with God; not just sin, sinning, and sinners. At this church, my curiosity for religion grew. So any down time I had, was spent studying the bible and attending church. Yes, the same person who hated going to church when I was younger was voluntarily going. I was purposely looking for a church activity every day of the week. It didn't matter which church; I just had to be in someone's church. I was yearning for knowledge. It had become addictive.

At age 25, I decided that my relationship with God meant more to me than a relationship with a woman (or man). To me, that meant suppressing those physical desires. Most people would say that I'm not being true to myself. That I'm allowing religion to control me. Yes, I am. That's a decision I made because I know the results of my obedience. Now, I'm not saying that being gay is a sin. I'm not saying that it's wrong and unnatural to love who you love. I am saying that for me, being in a physical relationship with a woman obstructs the relationship I have with God. This may not be the case for everyone...I can only speak for myself.

Am I happy? Yes. Everyone's relationship and walk with God are different. I wholeheartedly believe this is His plan and purpose for me.

Are there some days I struggle? Yes. I'm human and still attracted to women. It's who I am and that won't change. My mentor and I are still very intimate with one another, although it has been seven years since we have been physical. Having an intimate relationship with someone is different from having a physical relationship. As I said before, physical relationships distract me from my purpose. Is possible to have an intimate relationship with someone you're not romantically involved with.

A year and a half ago, I celebrated my 10-year high school reunion. Many of my classmates are still in that in between stage of life, so it still shocks me that I have accomplished so much in only a few years; all because of my obedience. Because of my position, I'm often asked to speak at youth related events. Some days I do it wearing a dress and heels; some days I'm wearing a three-piece suit, necktie, and oxfords. Either way, I'm touching the lives of so many young people who remind me of myself.

Today, I am who I'd never imagined I'd become: a minister, writer, entrepreneur, and corporate executive. Once I completely gave my life to God, EVERYTHING fell into place. I would say I prayed for this, but I didn't. My prayer was to become all of who God ordained me to be. So here I am: still gay, still Christian, and still passing as straight.

NikoJoe Arnold,

Co-Author

Nikojoe is the Co-Author of "Passing as Straight". She is also authoring another project called "Art of Mastering Me". She's a mother of three one son D'Vontis 26, two daughters Chyna 21 and Trahuna 17; she also has a granddog by the name Roxanne. She was raised in Opa-locka FL, she reside in (Atlanta, GA). Nikojoe is the owner of Vintage Missfit online thrift boutique. She has hopes of becoming a real-estate tycoon. Before Nikojoe became Nikojoe she was Nicole a troubled young single mother who looked in all the wrong places for acceptance and love. She's always had dreams and goals but has always let fear and naysayers control her way of thinking. Niko's goals include being on New York's bestseller list an Author of many books, mentoring future adults, having a nonprofit to help single young mothers to continue their education, getting into real estate and being the voice and vessel of the *Art of Mastering Me*. Her Favorite songs include "Master piece" By: Jasmine Sullivan and "Get up 10" by: Cardi B" Niko believes in the universe, manifestation and affirmation. She enjoys mediating, reading, dancing and riding bikes. Some of her favorite quotes include, "I'm a dreamer"

"I Dream with my eyes wide open" ~ Unknown

Favorite color is turquoise it has meanings of refreshing, feminine, calming, sophisticated, energy, wisdom, serenity, wholeness, creativity, emotional balance, good luck, spiritual grounding, friendship, love, joy, tranquility, patience, intuition, and loyalty.

Favorite scripture: Matthew 7
Instagram: @nikojoe, @vintagemissfit, & @artofmasteringme
Facebook: Nikojoe Arnold

Art of Mastering Me

by NikoJoe Arnold

You would think in 2020 nobody would care about your sexuality right? Well guess what they care and it's still a big thing to some, you lose friends, respect, you don't get that promotion, hell some jobs won't hire you and family members,

"Shit" they just disown you.

Let me start off first by saying "I am not a victim" my situation with men has nothing to do with my sexuality" hell I was the problem in most of my heterosexual relationships "shrugs" well maybe not all but some lol. I did have this one crazy dude but still that situation has nothing to do with me being a lesbian. Also let me be clear this is not a phase, as soon as someone hears you're gay they automatically assume it's a phase. Because of my age I'm considered a late bloomer… I would like to think at 41 years old I know what I want!

Society is the reason most people stay in the closet. If you don't know the *"Art of Mastering Me"* the comments and the stares will drive, you insane. The world treats you like being gay is a disease, they treat you like your sexuality is contagious, like if you hang with me you're going to catch being gay. Or the judgmental ones that don't want to be around you because you're gay and they think the saying "birds of a feather flock together" is true, but that is not a true statement. I've sat in a room full of people before, listening to how they feel about someone being gay and I felt so alone. Let me be very clear homophobic comments about men offend a woman who's passing as straight as well. Many young people have been so afraid to come out they have committed suicide, ran away from home, and turned to drugs. You have some that have been put out on the streets because of their sexuality and that just breaks my heart. It's not easy *"passing as straight"*! It's very hard to live a double life. It's hard to love someone while hiding. It's hard to feel like you're in a bubble all by yourself. It's one thing to be private but to be afraid of who you are a different ball game. My kids finding out was a breeze...

I tried to hide it from them; they were actually the first to find out my two daughters Chyna and Trahuna. I use to be on the phone all the time something I rarely did, when they would come in my room I'll try to act like I wasn't on the phone or I was on the phone with a friend or a dude, until finally they were fed up with me and said "omg ma we know you be on the phone with a girl we know you gay and nobody cares! Eventually my son found out and he was mad that I hide it from him. Just like that I was out to my kids. My kids were never my concern because I raised my kids with a solid foundation, I raised them not to judge, and I didn't raise them in a box. My concern was my momma. My mom is an Old Testament reading Christian with no filter she says whatever out her mouth. When I say the lady didn't play, I mean it. I was scared to tell her... ok I admit I was terrified. My mom still doesn't accept me being lesbian, but she does accept me if that makes since.

I dated men at a distance and when I say distance, I mean no Thanksgiving no Christmas and you sure wasn't meeting my mom. Meeting my ole girl is a privilege. The things I use to do to hide my true sexuality man oh man. I stayed in an abusive relationship for years trying to conceal my sexuality. Every failed attempted at being straight caused so much stress on my body and me. I used to go out almost every night get drunk possibly leave with someone then disappear, I've met men ran in to them again and didn't remember meeting them. I used to drink myself sick trying to be this perfect straight person. Keeping my life private from my family caused some in the family to speculate "Nikki gay". Chile guess who cursed everybody out? You better believe it, me when I say I cursed everybody out I mean it! I no longer wanted to be around my family because of the chatter but I still denied it. I used to say man I'm not eating no 'coochie' a woman can't do shit for me yawl got me messed up. The whole time I had me an ole young thang (stud) but still afraid and in the closet. Now get this momma met her and all but she still wasn't with it though. My first actual lesbian relationship was good but when it got bad it was horrible. So, you can only imagine when we broke up the comments I got "Oh that was a phase" momma was like thank God that's over, but honestly, I couldn't be that mad at them because I egged it on agreed with them. I had one foot out the closet and one foot in, then I stepped right back in.

I tried to date men again and I remember feeling like something was missing. When I dated men, I craved a woman. But when I dated a woman, I never craved a man. I remember saying after my first situation I would never date women again. All the while I knew that wasn't true it just sounded good at the moment and I was still trying to please everyone but me. I used to sit on the phone for hours with my cousin April telling her how I felt, letting her know my struggles (April knows the good, the bad and the ugly about me she's my dairy).

When I finally decided I can't pretend anymore I still allowed my fear to become "self-proclaimed non-gender specific" I use to walk around saying "I like what I like". So, at that point I didn't consider myself bisexual because I didn't cross crafts meaning I didn't date both at the same time, but even with that -- meeting men and women I was still missing something. I was still pretending, I wasn't happy, and I was still trying to please everyone. I ended up falling into depression. I didn't have an appetite; I couldn't sleep I was in a really dark place. Until one day I attended this event last minute, I met this lady. We met through mutual friends and would sit and talk for hours. When we met, we both had been through some things, so we really weren't looking for anyone. We both agreed to take our time so we can get things right. Our chemistry was amazing. I thought I knew what I wanted in women before I met her, but I was wrong. Her touch, her eyes, the way her mouth moves as she articulated her words, it was just something about her that was different. I finally found someone who understood me battling with my sexuality, she understood me passing as straight. She never pressured me to do or say anything. She was so patient with me and understanding. She taught me things about myself I didn't know. She gave me the push I needed with her kind words and support to finally live my truth. Most importantly she did not try to put me in a box! Most people I've met would love the person they met until they fell in love. Once they fell in love I was put in a box. They didn't like that carefree full of life Niko, the MF's tried to turn me into mother Theresa. But she didn't that lady loved me just as I am -- loud goofy full of life Niko. She gave me balance because we are totally different. She is really cool and laid back and as for me I am free as a bird.

The *__Art of Mastering Me__* came when I started to not care, I stopped worrying about people, I started living for me and doing things that made me happy. I began to feel like new money, man my edges came back, I was starting to rest more, ass got bigger, and I started walking around with an S on my chest with my head high! I was walking around like Bitch I'm back!

When I walk the song that plays in my head is "we made it" by rap artist Drake. Now that I'm living freely as a lesbian woman it's now new battles to face. You have friends that feel like you want them or wanted them the whole time. Then you have the friends that think because you're out now you should've started a relationship with them. You also have the ones that are now still your friend but act totally different with you like because you're gay you're not the same ole Niko anymore. Well let me be the first to let you know being a lesbian is no different from being heterosexual. It works the same way! In a heterosexual relationship you look for attraction you have a certain type! Guess what it's the same with being a lesbian you have a type "WE DONT WANT EVERY GIRL THAT PASSES OUR WAY" Thank you! So, stop with the shenanigans. Guys are the worse at times. I've gotten DM's "how you know you gay if you never tried me" or the famous "she can't do what I do" oh and my most recent one "you will be coming back to 'D' soon".

Have you ever seen a couple and their chemistry lights up the whole room? Well that's bae and me. When bae and I are out we demand attention when we walk in a room because of our chemistry we get a lot of smiles and blushes but other times we get frowns. The men just stare and shake their heads!!!! The worst thing you can do is stare at me I'll give that ass something to look at tongue all down her throat! "Giggles"

This book was created to help everyone not just women, this book is for down low men as well because they have it just as bad or even worse. The title for women is passing as straight, but some may compare it to men on the down low. It's so many men that will love to live in their truth but can't because of fear of losing everything and it's sad. Sexuality should not determine who you are. Sexuality should not be based on looks (you're too pretty to be gay), like what does gay look like? It should not determine your qualifications on a job. Family shouldn't think you're different because of your sexuality. Gay, straight or other equals human we are all still human!

Repeat after me "I am amazing, I am me, I am living my truth, I am more than enough, I can love who I choose.

Be you be free!

Shyheta Johnson,

Co-Author

I am Shyheta Johnson I am 34 years old I am a hearing-impaired activist a CBD advocate a Total Life Changer. I am on a mission to change many lives around the globe. I'm also a crochet designer and a mother of five children. Despite the chaotic events taking place I'm my life I live by the motto what doesn't kill you makes you stronger.

I have faced many burdens alone, so I was given the name "sturdy sista". I love to make people smile and laugh - I know that laughter is medicine for the soul.

Instagram: @iamshyhetamonroe

The Lonely Secret

by Shyheta Johnson

They say that when life throws you lemons work hard to make lemonade from them.

This is a short story about me coming out as bisexual, after pretending to be straight for a long time.

I am Shyheta Johnson. I am a thirty-four years old, African American woman bisexual single mother living in Philadelphia.

One other important information you must know about me is that I am hearing impaired. Yes, you heard that right. I can't hear at all, and I advocate for other women who have this same disability.

Growing up was tough for me. My parents were never married, neither did they live together. Most of my family members - including my mother, didn't relate to me because of my hearing disability. I was like a plague they were ashamed to have, and this was a big emotional challenge for me.

I grew up shuttling between different homes including that of my mom and dad. Because I am hearing impaired and from a poor background, I had to drop out of school early and rely on educating myself in other ways.

At about the age of twelve through thirteen my mother's boyfriend was using me to sell crack cocaine in the streets of Philadelphia. I was a perfect courier for his small cartel as most police officers hardly suspected young females, let alone a popularly known deaf one.

At age thirteen, I lost my father. He was murdered when I was in a juvenile detention center so; I couldn't even attend his burial.

To date, no one knows who killed him or why he was killed.

So, imagine me selling crack for my mother's boyfriend, and living in a home where no one gave a damn about me. My mother had children with this man, but he'd send me out into the streets selling drugs to all sorts of crooks. I was just twelve damn it.

I had to grow up fast to fend for myself since no one cared about me.

I have shared my background in detail so that you can understand the place I am coming from.

I am not ashamed of my past, this journey made me who I am today and helped me grow into the woman I am now.

I have read stories of how the tide turned for different people, but I am not lucky to be amongst this set of people.

My life progressed faster than it should have.

There is a lot I want to write about now in this book, but the details are just too much to fill the pages of my section.

I'll probably write those details subsequently in another book.

I grew up around people with a lot of religious and cultural backgrounds.

Like I said earlier, I am black, and I grew up in an urban neighborhood where people held a lot of beliefs as to what is right or wrong.

Even at the various foster homes where I stayed at different times, there were strictly religious and so-called moral beliefs that were enforced.

Bear in mind that all I learned growing up about sexual relationships was from the contemporary man and woman's point of view.

I couldn't hear the discussions and warnings since I am deaf, but I could read a little. I read newspapers at our local church on the concept of homosexuality, bisexuality, etc. which often painted these people as bad, possessed, insane or something worse.

My journey to self-discovery started in one of the foster homes. As a thirteen-year-old girl, I was already blossoming physically. My breasts were just beginning to form nice contours, and my curves were beginning to take shape. My round face was a delight to look upon. To summarize my looks, it is safe to say I looked attractive to both men and women. I was aware that men were attracted to me, but I didn't notice the female attraction initially.

On a very sunny afternoon one day, I was alone with one of the girls who shared my dorm with me named Katy (not her real name). That afternoon, I dodged a program that was meant for all the children at the home and snuck back to the dorm bathroom. It was a surprise when Katy snuck into the bathroom too and we were all alone in the bathroom. Katy was one of the more outgoing girls in the dorm, and she was older than me by a few years.

We started talking since we were already familiar with each other, and it didn't take long before we became comfortable talking with each other. When Katy started asking personal questions about my sexual life, I felt awkward initially. But over time, she was able to persuade me to open up about my escapades.

Later on, during the talk, Katy suddenly asked if I had ever been with a female in a sexual way to which I responded to in the negative.

Katy moved closer towards me, and before I could blink an eye, she began running her hands over my body.

Although I couldn't tell what she was doing, I could see the fire of desire that burnt in her gaze.

Initially, I tried resisting her because the experience was feeling weird, but when her hand started traveling to intimate places and I started to feel electricity run down my spine. We ended up kissing and touching each other for a while.

This was my first near sexual experience with a female. We would have gone beyond this that day because I was in so much pleasure that I let my guard down for Katy, but she suddenly stopped and signaled to me that the program was over and our dorm mates were returning.

After this day, I realized that I wasn't only attracted to men alone, but that I loved women as much as I loved men, and even much more.

After this experience, curiosity got the best of me, and I wanted to know more. I would check out girls, but this didn't mean that I rejected the advances of boys. The boys got my attention, but the girls made me feel as hot as the boys did.

I kept the experience I shared with Katy to myself for years, and even after I left the foster home, I didn't disclose it to anyone. I had to act like every other girl I knew. I was a hearing-impaired girl who was barely accepted, and I knew whatever little acceptance I got from people would vanish if they knew I was bisexual.

Most of the bisexuals that I read about were already stigmatized and I didn't want people to see me as they saw them.

This stigmatization is the reason I had to act straight and not bisexual, and I held on to this illusion for years.

I stopped selling drugs years later when I met Mr. Wayne (not his real name). I was just sixteen, young, dumb and broke, and I didn't think before I started sleeping with him.

He was old enough to be my father and to make matters worse, his mother didn't approve of the relationship or us living together.

During my time with Mr. Wayne, I would run into ladies that tickled my fancy. Women that made me pause and take a second look because I was attracted to them in more ways than just friendship, but I couldn't act on any of this.

What would people think of me? I'd think. I was barely accepted because of my different abilities, so I was scared that coming out, as bisexual would make people accept me even less.

One day we went to a strip club called "The Box".

A lesbian called Coco kept peeping in the box where I was, and her stares made me hot. Coco later approached me. She made a pass at me from her suggestive touches. Coco was my kind of woman, a woman who worked and had a motorcycle – which is sexy as hell to me, and very beautiful. I turned her down that night because Wayne was waiting outside, and I knew he would make a scene if he found me getting so close too Coco.

I ended up having two kids for Wayne though we never got married. How could we? He was very controlling, he acted like I was a property he owned and almost ruined my life.

After my second child, Wayne was arrested and after the prosecution, he was sent to prison.

During Wayne's incarceration, I had my 4th child by a new man.

I never mentioned or showed my sexuality to any of these men while we were together.

To them, I was a straight woman, but I knew I was a bisexual just acting straight to be accepted and to have my needs met.

It was quite unfortunate that the government took my three kids away leaving me to be all alone. This is a story for another day.

All through my time with Wayne and subsequently other men, I had fantasies of being with women.

I would dream about a popular female singer in America – I won't mention her name. Every time I saw her on TV, or I heard her voice come up, it would turn me on greatly. I don't know if she's into women sexually, but she was one of my sexual fantasies. Time passed, and I moved on. Memories of the moments I spent with Katy at thirteen kept flooding my mind every time I was sexually involved with somebody.

It was like my body was yearning to relive the moment, begging me to find an avenue for that day to reoccur again. The best way to explain this period is to simply say I found it impossible to imagine or concentrate on sleeping with men alone. Because of my hearing impairment, it was and it's still a little difficult for me to meet new people and get to know them easily. Not everyone understands sign language, and not everyone has time to write a lot down for you to read and comprehend. I would have opted for Internet dating, but I wasn't that desperate yet.

My journey to coming out as bisexual finally began when I met Chanel. Although slightly older than me, Chanel is the definition of a black goddess beauty. Due to my finances not being set up right and some other personal reasons, I had to move to a new neighborhood once more.

I moved to a new one in Pottstown PA, and it is at this place that I met Chanel. She was a single mother with two kids, but she had a man - who I later got to know was her baby daddy - who visited regularly.

I would fantasize about Chanel in private, and I never imagined we could ever become friends or lovers. First, I didn't know she was bisexual, and secondly, she looked out of my league. Things, however, took a wild turn after some months of my arriving at Pottstown PA.

Chanel must have noticed me constantly admiring her or spotted me glancing lustfully at her. How it happened next -- exactly, I don't remember.
What I know is that she began to return my glances, and later, she would wave in greetings. Not long afterward,

Chanel began visiting me at home over time, and that's how we became friends.

It is difficult to explain how our relationship started. Chanel is not very vast in sign communication, but somehow, we got along. We started exchanging late night text and chat, which later grew into flirting. One Friday morning, she came over to my place. One thing led to another, and what happened next is etched in my memory as one of the most amazing sexual encounters I have ever had.

I may decide to put details of this encounter in some other book -- they are too raw for this one you are holding.

From that day forward, I would meet with Chanel regularly and we would have steaming sex together. Later on, Chanel's baby's father started joining our escapades. We would have threesomes together, and sometimes Chanel's baby's father would have sex with me while Chanel watched.

People started noticing our extra closeness, and people started to talk. Although I couldn't hear any of these talks, the cold shoulder and frowns I was beginning to get from a few people, started telling me their reactions toward me wasn't like before.

I later found out that I was a screamer in bed, and I guess my moans of ecstasy was how her neighbors got to know that I was having sex with Chanel.

Also, I later found out that some people knew Chanel's sexual status already, and these people didn't find it too hard to connect the dots when they saw us together. They too were instrumental in spreading the word about my sexuality. Several things happened between Chanel and myself that are no stories for this book.

Of notable mention are events such as the fact that Chanel's baby's father later wanted me and him to have a relationship behind her back, which I refused immediately. Also, Chanel is a crazy woman. She had her child's father, me as a sidepiece and a boyfriend.

There was this one time when her boyfriend caught us making love in her room. I was scared to the bones and a fight ensued. I didn't need to have two ears to know that the argument was loud which attracted unnecessary attention. A fight broke out that day, and Chanel's boyfriend would have stabbed me if it were not for the skills I had picked up in my drug-dealing days.

Thankfully, I sustained only minor injuries and no life was lost. This event was one of the ways my sexuality became known to some other people. At this point, I was beginning to get stigmatized in my neighborhood, but I was yet to come out as bisexual.

I'd like to mention at this point that I took care of Chanel's children like they were my own. It was like I was compensating for the three I lost by treating her children like my own.

Things finally went south between Chanel and me when she tried to poison me. I don't know if she did it out of jealousy or anger that her baby daddy was beginning to like me more, but she tried poisoning me and I found out.

This was how I ended my first major bisexual relationship.

It is worth mentioning that around the time that I was sleeping with Chanel, I was also sleeping with another man.

There was a particular police detective I was having sex with then, but I didn't come out as bisexual to him or any other person for that matter.

Most men don't like sharing what they believe to be theirs with anyone, so coming out as bisexual might have been a recipe for disaster.

Not long after I left Chanel, I met another woman I call Punchy.

We attended the same cooking class, and over time, we became close. Her husband was sick and because I was a little free, I'd go over to her place to help her out. I found out she was bisexual later, and we had sex one time together. But like Wayne, she too was possessive. She'd lock the door and pretend to have lost the keys just to keep me indoors, and she was always taking advantage of my hearing impairment. The moment I was free from her, I left and never returned.

Punchy was the second woman I had a relationship with, but I was still ashamed to declare my sexual orientation to anyone. The fact that I had now been with two women who misbehaved severely during the relationships was also one of the reasons I was keeping my sexual orientation to myself.

Another time I was with a woman was when I met Asia. Asia is a single mother of two, five years younger than me, and she was a beauty too.

I met Asia at a party through her aunt and we became friends almost instantly. Asia was gentler and more understanding than any of the women I have ever been with. I enjoyed her company more than I did with Chanel or Punchy. The sex with her was also very mind-blowing, and she introduced me to more avenues for pleasure. Word had spread at this time, and I was beginning to have to constantly deal with people trying to judge me because of my sexuality.

You can't run from whom you are - or can you? I was going through emotional and mental stress during this period. Why couldn't I just be myself and be proud of it? Was I going to live my life constantly in fear of what people thought of me? All these questions were the constant imagination that filled my heart.

Unlike the other two women I had met earlier, she showed me that there are loving women out there. Women who wouldn't take advantage of you or try to treat you like a piece of property. Asia was always kind to me, understanding, and she always accepted me for who I am.

Years later, I met another man and gave birth to two kids. Both kids are still with me to date. I didn't tell him that I was bisexual until recently. A few months later, I discovered this project through a woman named Kinyatta Gray.

When I heard about this book idea, I was encouraged to come out and share this secret with the world. Since I was getting more comfortable being myself and I was beginning to get less bothered by people's opinions, I decided to share my lonely secret. So, I started with my baby's father first. I was surprised when he said there was nothing wrong with being bisexual. He was ok with it.

Isn't it amazing that one of the persons I was so scared wouldn't accept me for my sexuality didn't even feel bothered about it at all? Maybe I would have told him earlier if I summoned enough courage. I also told my daughter's godmother because she is such an angel. She has always loved us for us and she wasn't judgmental even after I told her I was bisexual.

I am no longer ashamed to share my lonely secret with the world. I no longer hide my sexuality on social media and tell it to anyone who cares to listen, or the ones who think they are in a position to condemn or judge me for who I am.

I'll leave you with these last words. If you are gay, lesbian, or bisexual, understand that this is nature at work. You are no less of a human being.

People will always act strangely and find it difficult to understand you - especially people who are not like you. Ignore the comments and live your life.

Remember, life is too short to be dying in silence by keeping lonely secrets. The world is more exposed and people are fighting every day for the LGBTQ community.

Leave your hiding spot, let people know who you are, share your lonely secret with the world and be proud of it.

10 LGBTQ Quotes To Remember

1. "When all Americans are treated as equal, no matter who they are or whom they love, we are all **more** free."-~ Barack Obama

2. "There will not be a magic day when we wake up and it's now okay to express ourselves publicly. We make that day by doing things publicly until it's simply the way things are."~ Tammy Baldwin

3. "Like racism and all forms of prejudice, bigotry against transgender people is a deadly carcinogen. We are pitted against each other in order to keep us from seeing each other as allies. Genuine bonds of solidarity can be forged between people who respect each other's differences and are willing to fight their enemy together. We are the class that does the work of the world, and can revolutionize it. We can win true liberation." ~ Leslie Feinberg

4. "Please remember, especially in these times of group-think and the right-on chorus, that no person is your friend (or kin) who demands your silence, or denies your right to grow and be perceived as fully blossomed as you were intended. ~ Alice Walker

5. "Everybody's journey is individual. You don't know with whom you're going to fall in love. ... If you fall in love with a man, you fall in love with a man. The fact that many Americans consider it a disease says more about them than it does about homosexuality." ~ James Baldwin

6. "I don't want you to love me. I don't want you to like me. But I don't want you to beat me up and kill me. You don't have to like me, I don't care. But please don't kill me." ~ Kristin Beck

7. "I want to do the right thing and not hide anymore. I want to march for tolerance, acceptance, and understanding. I want to take a stand and say, "Me, too.'"
~ Jason Collins

8. "I am a strong, black, lesbian woman. Every single time I say it, I feel so much better." ~ Brittney Griner

9. I was raised in Holland, where race and homosexuality are not a subject matter but rather a part of life. ~ Yolanda Hadid

10. Tell me again how you think God will judge others for who they love, and not judge you for hating someone you've never met? ~Unknown

LGBTQ Resources

Workplace
https://outandequal.org
Legal
http://www.nclrights.org
Political
https://www.thetaskforce.org
Youth
https://www.glsen.org
Military
https://modernmilitary.org
Black Lesbian Love & Relationship Blog
https://www.blacklesbianlovelab.com
GLAAD
https://www.glaad.org/

Best Selling Author Kinyatta E. Gray's

Upcoming New Release (May 2020)

"From Section to C.E.O." is an epic and triumphant tale of courage, grit, and resilience about how a woman managed to navigate her most vulnerable times.

With nothing more but the desire to attain the "American Dream", this story follows Heaven, an intelligent, driven and determined lady who is more than capable of achieving everything she wants, but is plagued by one fatal flaw; the will to take shortcuts on her road to success.

Heaven's dream seemed to have found its form when she becomes pregnant and has a child for her high school sweetheart (the heir to a multimillion-dollar family fortune), and with it came the feeling that her dreams and perfect life would be all but secured.

Unfortunately, her nightmares were just about to begin.

Knowledge of her ethnicity causes Heaven not only to lose her dream life, but causes her man's family to disown him, thereby throwing a wrench in her already scripted, shortcut means to achieve all she ever dreamed about.

Doused in failure, lack, stagnation and suffering beyond anything she had ever imagined, Heaven finds herself seeking a way out of it all... a way to bring her pain to an end...

Scripted with courage, grace and rare insight, bestselling author "Kinyatta E. Gray" captures the epic panorama of a woman's worth, with her main intent being the desire to tell the heartbreaking story of a beautiful and resilient mother's spirit, in relation to women in general all around the world.

Best Selling Author

Kinyatta E. Gray's
Published (October 2019)

Losing a loved one is one of the hardest things we will ever have to face. But, imagine being the only child of an adopted mother and with no biological family to lean on when God calls her home. October 21, 2018 – the day Kinyatta's life as she once knew it would forever be changed, leaving her to embrace a new perspective on earth, alone. In this memoir, 30 Days: Surviving the Trauma and Unexpected Loss of a Single Parent as an Only Child, Kinyatta reflects on a 30-day period that changed the course of her life. She'll uncover some of her deepest pain, greatest joys, unspeakable trauma, and how she allowed love to heal. Kinyatta's honesty is brutal, but her truth is the only vessel that gives her hope to continue living the life that memorializes her mother's legacy.

TRAVELING GLAMOROUSLY
WILL ALWAYS BE IN STYLE

FLIGHTS IN Stilettos

KINYATTA GRAY
CREATOR AND CEO

@FStilettos
@flightsinstilettos
flightsinstilettos@gmail.com
flightsinstilettos.com

It's travel Season!

FlightsInStilettos® was founded in 2018 by Author and Celebrity Travel Influencer Kinyatta E. Gray. Kinyatta's goal is to inspire women to put their best selves forward when traveling and to identify their individual travel style. FlightsInStilettos offers women travel-inspired accessories and, apparel with a touch of glam as well as luxurious environmental friendly 100% microfiber Glam Girl Beach Towels!

CONSIDER FlightsInStilettos

ACCESSORIES, APPAREL, AND BEACH TOWELS WHEN PLANNING YOUR NEXT GIRL'S TRIP!

FLIGHTS IN Stilettos

Chyari

@FLIGHTSINSTILETTOS | @FSTILETTOS | MRSKINYATTA

VISIT WWW.FLIGHTSINSTILETTOS.COM

SEP 2019
LEADING WITH LEE
THE CEO TALKS BUSINESS START UP
FIRST LOOK:
ALEXANDRIA JEFFREY EXCLUSIVE
AUTUMN PICKS!
THE CEO BEHIND UPSCALE TAX LLC
FASHION GXD

the
DAVI
Magazine
"I was not always   on the path that
I'm on now, but one   day I made a
choice how I would   live my life
and what I wanted   in my life –
and once I made   those choices
everything   thereafter
became   a goal."
KINYATTA E. GRAY
FlightsInStilettos